The Longing Heart

Story of Abu Dhar

Khurram Murad

The Islamic Foundation

© The Islamic Foundation 1985/1405 H. Reprinted 1990/1410 H. and 2004
ISBN 0 86037 138 7

All rights reserved. No part of this publication may be reproduced, stored in a retrieval system or transmitted by any means whatsoever, without the prior permission of the copyright owner.

MUSLIM CHILDREN'S LIBRARY

General Editors:
Khurram Murad and **Mashuq Ally**

THE LONGING HEART

Author: **Khurram Murad**

Illustrations: **Hanife Hasan**

Editing: **Mardijah A. Tarantino**

These stories are about the Prophet and his Companions and, though woven around authentic ahadith, should be regarded only as stories.

Published by:
The Islamic Foundation,
Markfield Dawah Centre,
Ratby Lane, Markfield,
Leicester LE67 9RN,
United Kingdom

Quran House, P.O. Box 30611,
Nairobi, Kenya

P.M.B. 3193, Kano, Nigeria

British Library Cataloguing in Publication Data
Murad, Khurram
    The Longing Heart: story of Abu Dhar. —— (Muslim children's library; 17)
    1. Muhammad (*Prophet*) —— Juvenile literature
    I. Title   II. Series
    297'.63   BP75
    ISBN 0-86037-138-7

Printed by Ashford Colour Press Ltd, Gosport, Hants.

MUSLIM CHILDREN'S LIBRARY

An Introduction

Here is a new series of books, but with a difference, for children of all ages. Published by the Islamic Foundation, the Muslim Children's Library has been produced to provide young people with something they cannot perhaps find anywhere else.

Most of today's children's books aim only to entertain and inform or to teach some necessary skills, but not to develop the inner and moral resources. Entertainment and skills by themselves impart nothing of value to life unless a child is also helped to discover deeper meaning in himself and the world around him. Yet there is no place in them for God, who alone gives meaning to life and the universe, nor for the divine guidance brought by His prophets, following which can alone ensure an integrated development of the total personality.

Such books, in fact, rob young people of access to true knowledge. They give them no unchanging standards of right and wrong, nor any incentives to live by what is right and refrain from what is wrong. The result is that all too often the young enter adult life in a state of social alienation and bewilderment, unable to cope with the seemingly unlimited choices of the world around them. The situation is especially devastating for the Muslim child as he may grow up cut off from his culture and values.

The Muslim Children's Library aspires to remedy this deficiency by showing children the deeper meaning of life and the world around them; by pointing them along paths leading to an integrated development of all aspects of their personality; by helping to give them the capacity to cope with the complexities of their world, both personal and social; by opening vistas into a world extending far beyond this life; and, to a Muslim child especially, by providing a fresh and strong faith, a dynamic commitment, an indelible sense of identity, a throbbing yearning and an urge to struggle, all rooted in Islam.

The books aim to help a child anchor his development on the rock of divine guidance, and to understand himself and relate to himself and others in just and meaningful ways. They relate directly to his soul and intellect, to his emotions and imagination, to his motives and desires, to his anxieties and hopes – indeed, to every aspect of his fragile, but potentially rich personality. At the same time it is recognised that for a book to hold a child's attention, he must enjoy reading it; it should therefore arouse his curiosity and entertain him as well. The style, the language, the illustrations and the production of the books are all geared to this goal. They provide moral education, but not through sermons or ethical abstractions.

Although these books are based entirely on Islamic teachings and the vast Muslim heritage, they should be of equal interest and value to all children, whatever their country or creed; for Islam is a universal religion, the natural path.

Adults, too, may find much of use in them. In particular, Muslim parents and teachers will find that they provide what they have for so long been so badly needing. The books will include texts on the Quran, the Sunnah and other basic sources and teachings of Islam, as well as history, stories and anecdotes for supplementary reading. Each book will cater for a particular age group, classified into: pre-school, 5-8 years, 8-11, 11-14 and 14-17.

We invite parents and teachers to use these books in homes and classrooms, at breakfast tables and bedside and encourage children to derive maximum benefit from them. At the same time their greatly valued observations and suggestions are highly welcome.

To the young reader we say: you hold in your hands books which may be entirely different from those you have been reading till now, but we sincerely hope you will enjoy them; try, through these books, to understand yourself, your life, your experiences and the universe around you. They will open before your eyes new paths and models in life that you will be curious to explore and find exciting and rewarding to follow. May God be with you forever.

And may He bless with His mercy and acceptance our humble contribution to the urgent and gigantic task of producing books for a new generation of people, a task which we have undertaken in all humility and hope.

Khurram Murad
Director General

وما توفيقي إلا بالله

Abu Dhar, a member of the Ghifar tribe, looked out over the valley of Waddan and watched the Makkan caravan making its way northwards, slowly twisting and curving into the distance, towards the eastern provinces of the Roman Empire.

There was a time when the coming of a caravan was the most exciting event in his life.

The Ghifar tribe lived in the Waddan valley, which, although it had poor water and grazing grounds, was the exact location through which the Makkan caravans, laden with their many goods and riches, had to pass. And, Abu Dhar used to lead the youths of his tribe in raids on the trade caravans. Tribe members lived by what these caravans gave in the way of protection money. And if they were not willing to pay the price, then Abu Dhar, (or Jundub Ibn Junada, as he was known to his friends), this bright-eyed and bold youth, the most audacious of them all, knew where and when to strike; and no caravan, thanks to him, got away without paying its due. When, as often happened, the caravan men agreed on the spot to pay up, then he would join them, staying far into the night, sharing food and drink and listening to their tales, their descriptions of far-off cultures, and how people lived in the civilised lands of the Roman and Sassanid empires.

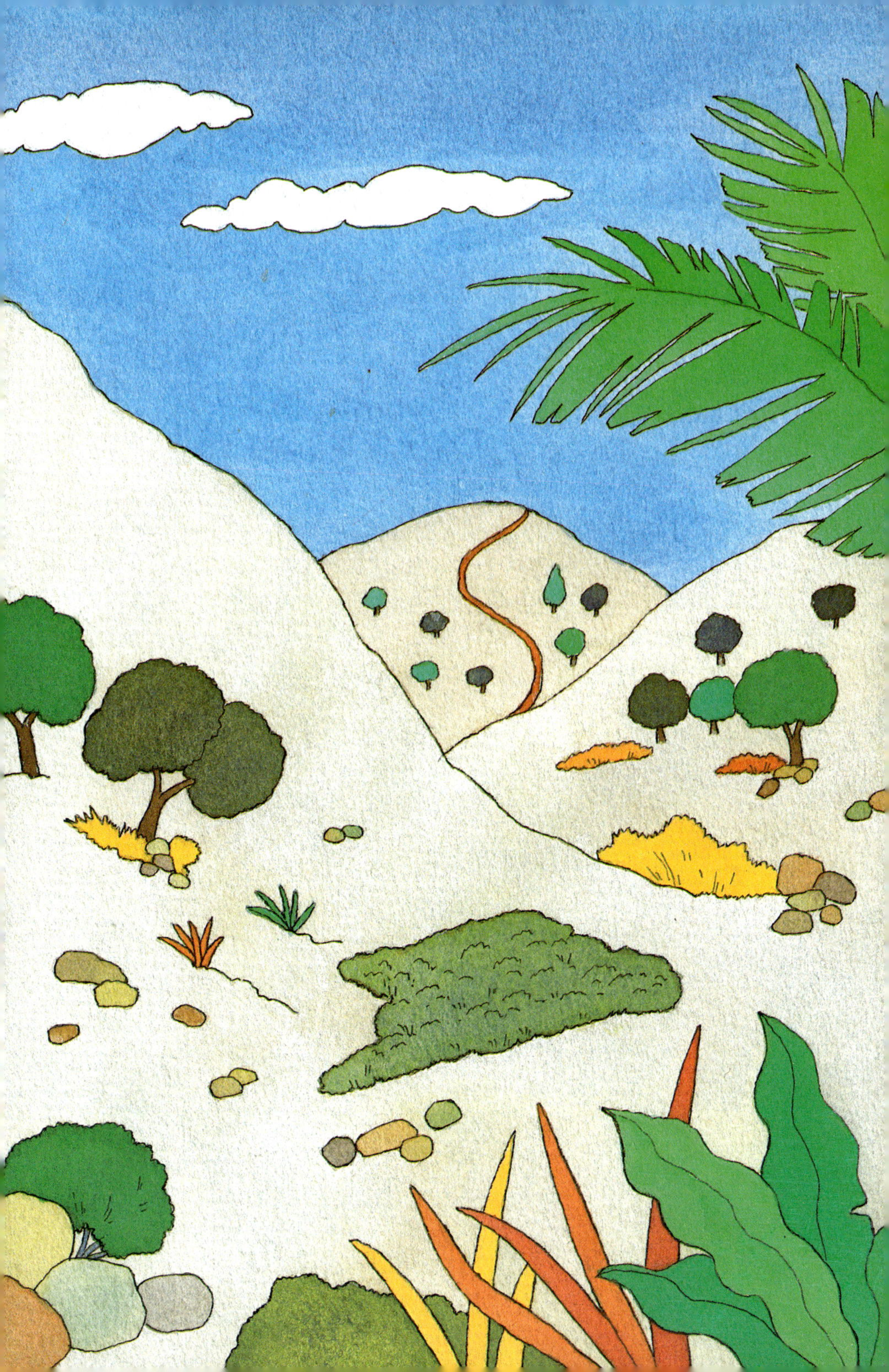

But now the exciting news was coming not from the mighty empires but from Makka, where a great upheaval was taking place. Makka was the spiritual and religious centre for all caravan drivers, and caravan raiders, too; it was also the hub and centre of all trade and commerce. News from Makka was therefore of much more concern to them than even the affairs of state in foreign provinces. So everyone had a view to express, and arguments on the new situation ran on and on. Abu Dhar was himself keenly interested in what was going on. That very morning, he had been talking with the caravan men, and none of them were in agreement. Some were saying that bad times had come to Makka, and were shaking their heads anxiously.

'The town has been turned upside down by a young rebel who wants to overthrow the gods of the Ka'ba and turn father against son, son against father. He brings great disruption', they complained.

As the daylight faded, another caravan man took Abu Dhar aside and spoke to him in whispers. 'This is not just an ordinary man, this Muhammad (Peace and Blessings be upon him).* He is from the respected tribes of the Quraysh, the Banu Hashim; and he claims to have received a message from the One God. He wants the people to give up worshipping idols and to submit to God, to Allah alone. I did not find him to be a bad man . . .', here, the caravan man

---

*Muslims are required to invoke Allah's blessings and peace upon the Prophet whenever his name is mentioned.

grew pensive, 'but the chiefs and the priests look upon him as a heretic and a fanatic. It seems only the young and the poor are joining him, one by one. Their devotion . . .', he said, laying a hand on Abu Dhar's arm, 'their devotion to him and to his cause makes up for their outer weaknesses'.

Abu Dhar was absolutely fascinated by this description of a man willing to risk all for the sake of his belief in One God. He found himself more and more intrigued. Some of the facts he heard haunted him that night, and he found himself suddenly awake, with certain phrases resounding in his heart, and mind, and ears. 'He worships but One God . . . he wishes to destroy the idols of Hubal and Al-Lat . . . mainly the young and the poor join him . . .' What sort of man would risk the enmity of a whole tribe? Who would encounter the anger of the elders of Makka for the sake of an idea . . . for the sake of One God . . . for what purpose would he cause himself so much trouble?, Abu Dhar asked himself. What could he gain from the adulation of a handful of poor, and young people? Where could all this lead but to eventual ruin or banishment? How could he know the truth about this man? With these questions running through his mind, he restlessly waited out the night.

At dawn, Abu Dhar's eager, intelligent face suddenly appeared at the door of his brother's tent.

'Anis', he called eagerly, 'listen to me. I cannot go to Makka myself, I have too much to do here, too many responsibilities. I want you to go for me. I want you to find out who this man Muhammad is, what his message is, and what he really wants. I trust your judgement, you are intelligent, you are also a poet. If this man's message is but poetry, you will know it. If you find that what he is reciting is worth listening to, then bring some of his words back to me.'

'As a matter of fact', responded Anis, 'I have been wondering about this man myself. How he has managed to cause so much trouble amongst the wise chieftains of the Quraysh, it amazes me. Listen, brother, I'll do as you suggest. I'll go for just a few days. That should give me time to discover something about him.'

So, taking a few dates, some dried meat and a sheep-skin bag of water, Anis set off down the valley by the southern route towards Makka.

For Abu Dhar, meanwhile, the hours and days passed as slowly as weeks and months. By the third day he was pacing back and forth between his tent and a look-out point to see if he could spot his brother coming home. That night, and the following night, he lay without sleep, expecting any moment to hear the padding of camel's feet announcing his brother's arrival.

'I should have gone myself', he grumbled. 'It would

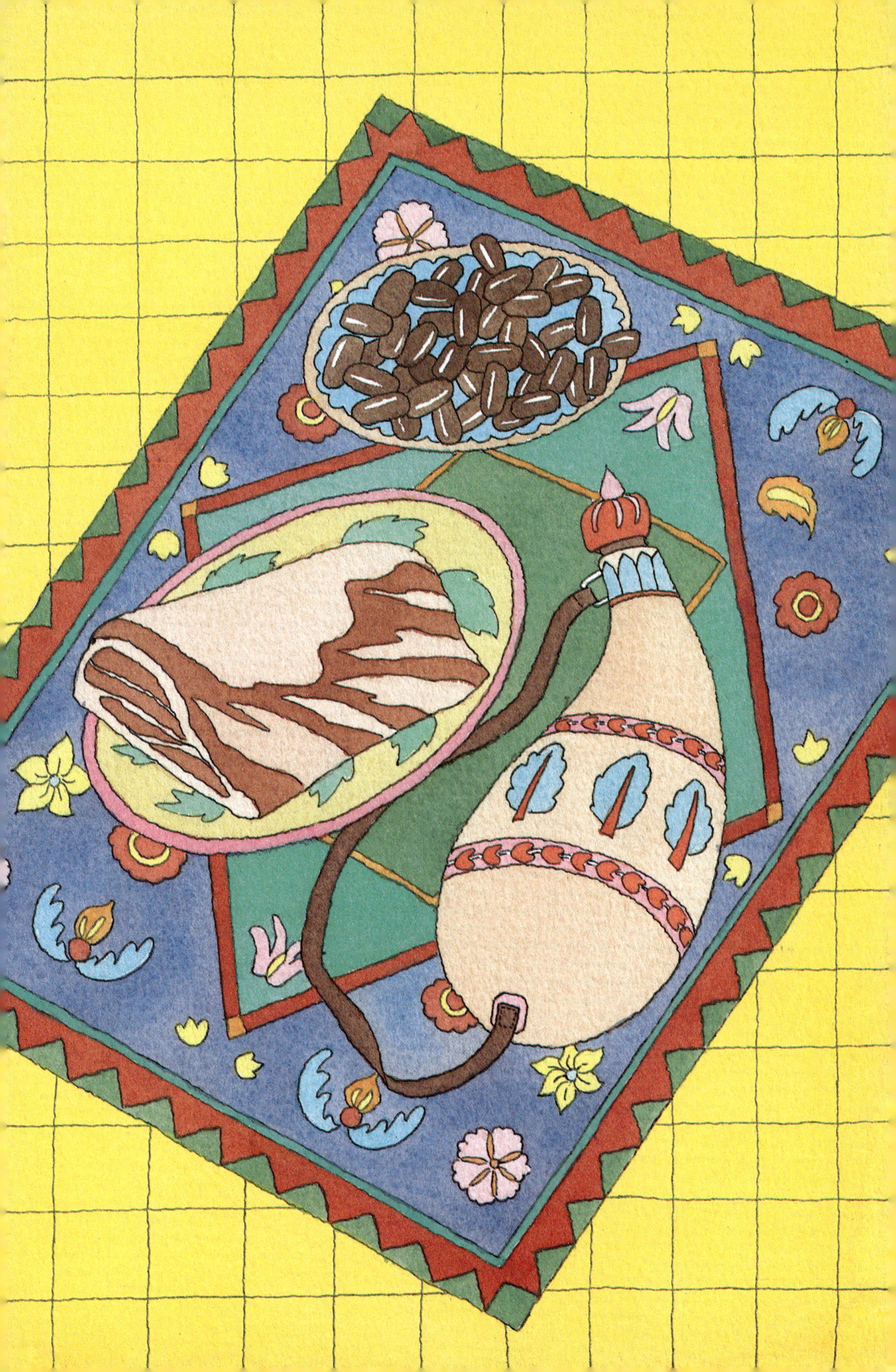

have been better than staying here. I have not been able to get any work done, anyway. But, then why should I care about what is happening in Makka? It is not even my town.'

At last, a week later, Anis arrived back from Makka. Abu Dhar embraced him and immediately began questioning him. 'Well . . . did you see him? Did you hear any of his verses? What does he speak of? What does he say about there being only One God?'

Anis smiled and brushed past his brother. 'I have been on a long journey at your request, at least let me wash and freshen up! And if you can bear to wait a moment longer, bring me something cool to drink.'

Once refreshed, Anis began his story. 'Well . . . I didn't get to see Muhammad, but I did hear some of his verses, which he says are not from him at all but from Almighty God, brought by the Archangel Gabriel. He declares that he is indeed the Messenger of One God. He says that we should worship no other gods but Him; only He is our Master, only Him should we serve. He hears whatever we say. He is with us wherever we are. That we should cleanse ourselves and pray; that we should make a point of doing good deeds and helping one another; and that we should feed the poor; and that we should not bury our girl children, that we should take care of widows and orphans. All this advice comes from him in the form of verse. Not the sort of verse I write, not what we usually know as poetry; yet in my opinion, it is far more beautiful than any poetry I have ever read in my whole life.'

'Is that so!' said Abu Dhar, who was hanging on every word his brother spoke. 'And the people, what do they say?'

'Well, of course', shrugged Anis, 'some accuse him of being just a poet and a show-off. Others say he is a soothsayer, kahen, like so many others; that he casts spells over people. And of course the Quraysh hate him for causing a disturbance. But I tell you, brother, what he utters is no ordinary poetry, he is no soothsayer. There is something in his message which is unlike anything anyone has ever said before.'

Abu Dhar sighed, rose to his feet and began pacing again, back and forth in front of his brother.

'I knew I should have gone myself', he moaned. 'Rather than feeling satisfied at what you are telling me, I am all the more drawn to this man. I will not be able to rest until I have met him.

Look, Anis, I have one more favour to ask of you.' Abu Dhar grabbed his brother by the shoulders and looked deeply into his eyes. 'I must go to Makka myself. Please, I ask you to look after my family while I am gone. Do this favour and you shall be rewarded for it, I swear.'

Anis smiled and spread open his arms. 'What was

the use of my going, then? Alright, brother, be on your way in peace. I can see nothing will stop you. Maybe you will be fortunate enough to hear his words from his own mouth. I'll look after your family while you are away. But be on your guard, the Makkans are in no mood to welcome followers of Muhammad.'

As soon as Abu Dhar entered the streets of Makka, he felt all was not as it should be. There was a tension in the air, and the inhabitants' faces showed signs of suspicion and mistrust. Everywhere there were little groups of people whispering about who had been the latest victim of persecution by the Quraysh, and what foolhardy act a follower of Muhammad had dared to commit.

He overheard how some had recited the verses too loudly, and had declared their faith in public places. He heard how one had refused to obey his parents, how another had stood face to face with his master and declared his faith in the One God. For all this, the followers of Muhammad were paying dearly. Many had done nothing to offend anyone, yet they were still being sought out and persecuted.

Abu Dhar realised that it might be dangerous to ask anybody about the Blessed Prophet. He might easily be considered a follower and be persecuted as were the others, and he was not ready yet to ally himself to a cause which he was not absolutely sure of.

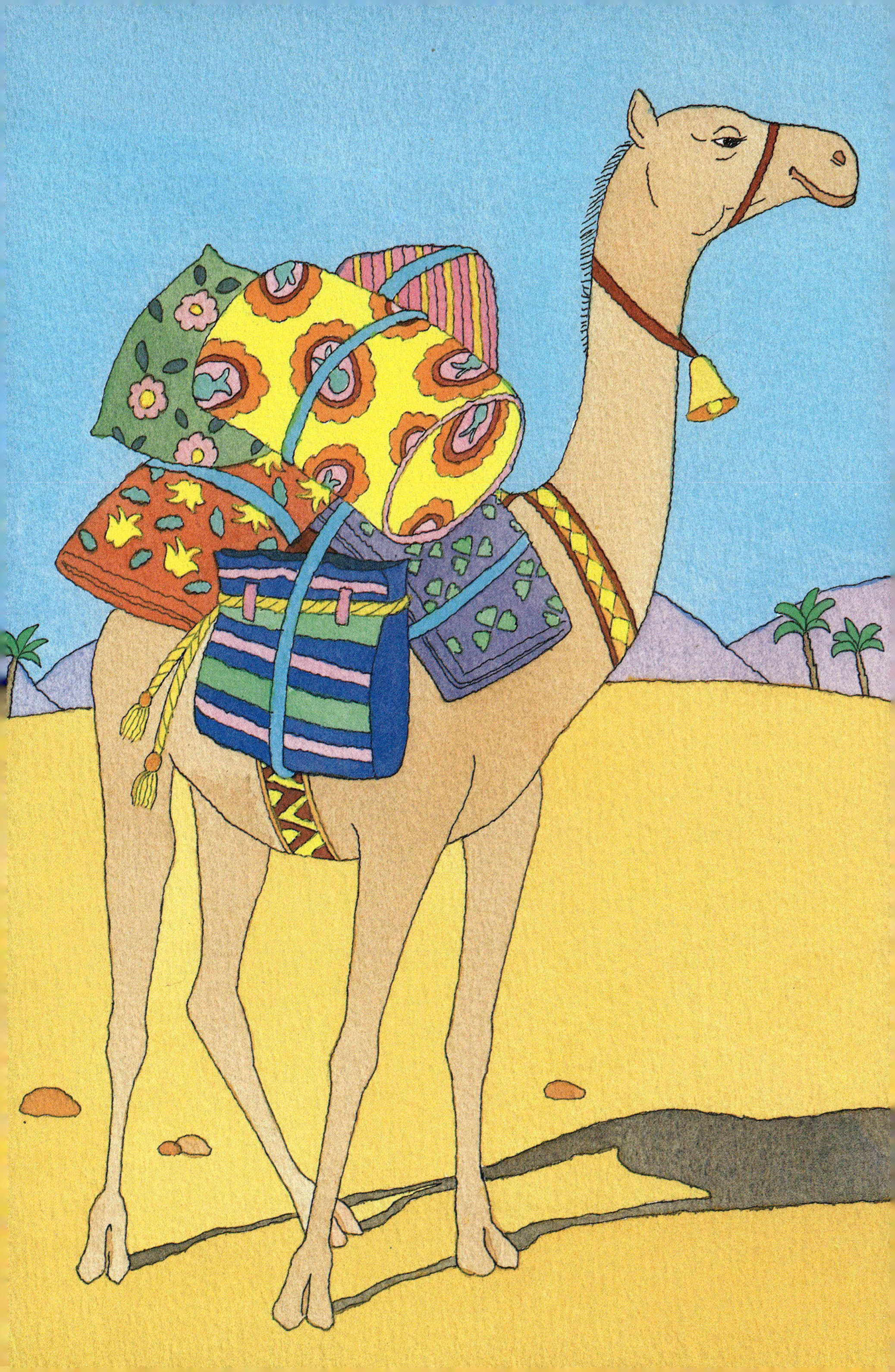

The Ka'ab, which stood in the centre of Makka, was not only the first structure to be consecrated to the worship of God, it also provided a shelter for those coming from far-away places on Pilgrimage. People from many different tribes rested there and left after a few nights. That was the natural place for Abu Dhar to make for after his long journey. No one spoke to him, and he was too weary to pay much attention to those around him.

Eventually, a young boy in his teens came by. He was dressed in well-worn clothes, but his smile was so warm and friendly when he spoke that Abu Dhar immediately took a liking to him.

'Greetings, stranger. You must have been on the road for days. How about joining me for a meal and a safe place to sleep?'

Abu Dhar was relieved. He knew no one in Makka, and he belonged to a tribe which could hardly be expected to have friends there. He got up and followed the boy to his home. On the way he asked: 'What is your name, son?'

'Ali', answered the boy.

'And mine is Abu Dhar. I'm from the Ghifar tribe in the valley of Waddan.'

Ali led him to his home, gave him something to eat and drink, and prepared a place for him to sleep. All this without asking Abu Dhar any questions about his purpose in coming to Makka.

The next morning, with a fresh supply of dates and water, Abu Dhar set off for the Ka'ba.

Another long day passed, and still Abu Dhar heard no mention of Muhammad's name, nor was there any sign of his followers. When evening came, he looked up and was surprised to see Ali approaching.

'So, here you are again', said Ali. 'Tell me, where do you want to go? I would be pleased to lead you there.'

Abu Dhar shook his head and looked away, not daring to confide in the boy.

'Never mind', Ali continued, 'come home with me again, you are very welcome'.

So Abu Dhar followed Ali to his house and spent a second night there. But still he hadn't the courage to ask Ali the whereabouts of a certain Muhammad.

All the next day he roamed the streets, trying to listen in on other people's conversations, trying to glean a bit of information as to which direction he should take, which part of town he should investigate, but not a clue came his way.

Wearily, he headed back to the Ka'ba, and as he had half-hoped, Ali appeared again as if it had been

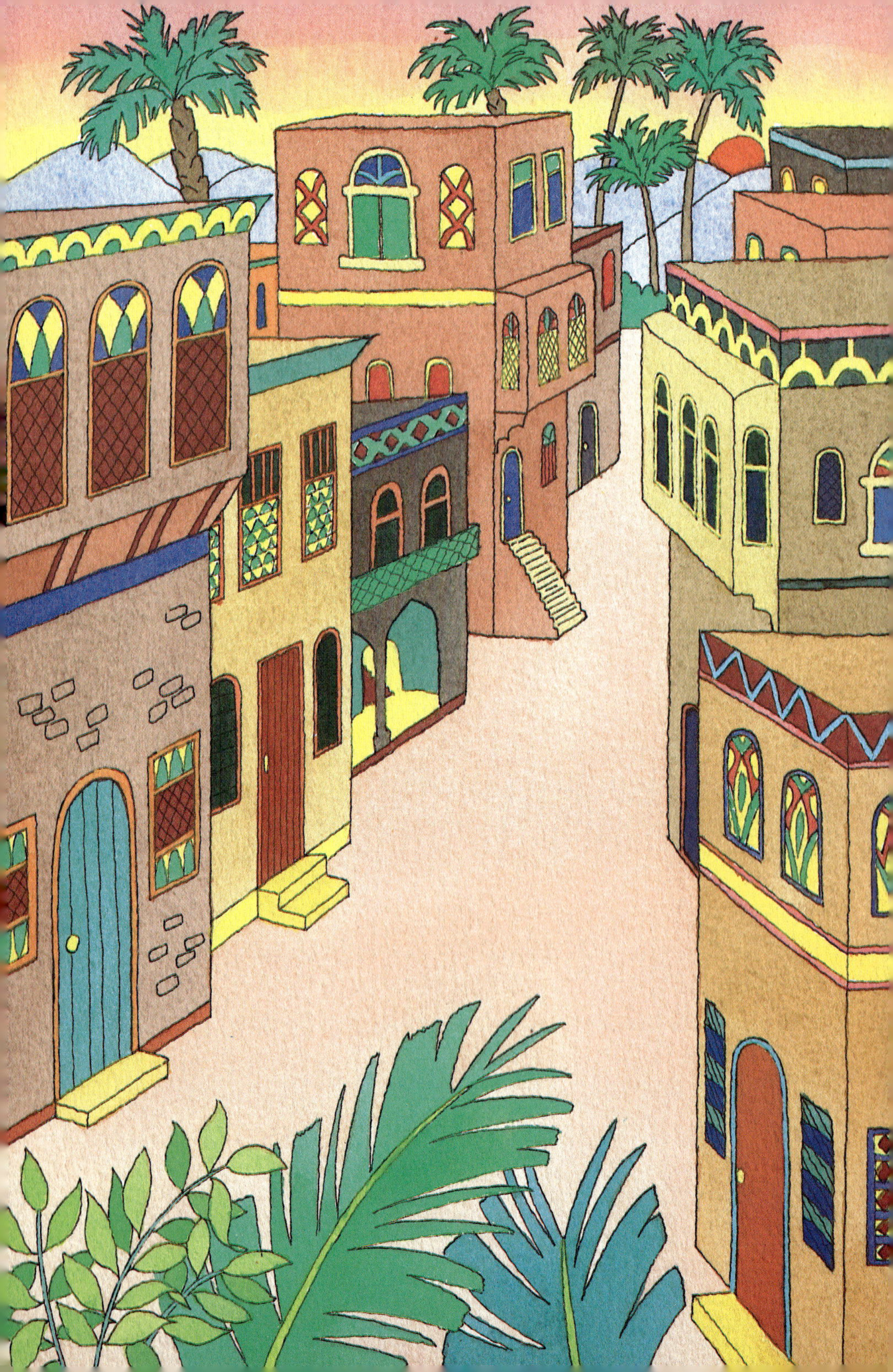

planned, and Abu Dhar accompanied him for the third time to his house.

They ate together, but neither one said more than a few words. Finally the youth smiled and leaned forward towards his guest. 'You see, there is nothing to fear here. You can trust me and I would be very happy if I could help you. Now tell me, what has brought you to Makka?'

Abu Dhar hesitated. He took a long drink of water, stared at the tumbler in his hand, and set it down in front of him. He was not sure what to do. Finally he reasoned that it was no use keeping quiet about his purpose, since he was getting nowhere wandering about the streets, waiting for information which never came. He was silly to be so cautious when it was obvious that this youth meant him no harm. He decided to speak:

'Alright', he said. 'But first give me your word that you will guide me to the person I want to see.'

'I will', promised Ali.

'I am seeking the new Prophet. The one who speaks about the One God.' Ali let out a cry of astonishment. 'I knew it!' he exclaimed, and his face lit up, 'I had a feeling that you were here for no ordinary purpose. You have come to the right place. Yes, of course I shall lead you to the Blessed Prophet! Yes indeed, he is the true Messenger of God, there is no doubt about it.'

Abu Dhar let out a sigh of relief as Ali continued on a more sombre note. 'Look, in the morning you shall come with me, but you must follow my instructions carefully, otherwise it could be dangerous for both of us. Always follow a few paces behind me. When I walk, you walk, when I stop, you stop, and when the danger passes, follow me. Enter whatever doorway or passage you see me enter.'

Abu Dhar nodded at these instructions, and the two then prepared for sleep.

But sleep did not come to Abu Dhar. All night long he tossed and turned. He could not believe what was happening to him. What he had hoped for was finally coming to pass, what he had travelled such a long distance for was finally within his grasp. Makka was a small town, only a few thousand people lived there, yet what a barrier there was to the way of the Blessed Prophet! Not only was the Messenger exiled within his home grounds, but barriers far more formidable, invisible barriers of hatred, ignorance and prejudice surrounded him. One could not be a coward if one wanted to approach him, and Abu Dhar knew within his heart, that in spite of the dangers his destination was finally in sight.

He was yearning, now, to hear with his own ears the verses and the advice from the Quran. He could not wait to meet the Blessed Prophet and hear of these revelations first hand, so that he could savour their meaning and fully understand their message.

بسم الله الرحمن الرحيم
الحمد لله رب العالمين ۞ الرحمن
الرحيم ۞ مالك يوم الدين ۞
اياك نعبد واياك نستعين ۞
اهدنا الصراط المستقيم
صراط الذين انعمت عليهم
غير المغضوب عليهم
ولا الضالين

The dreary hours of night dragged on, while Abu Dhar waited with anticipation for the dawn.

At last daylight came, and soon the sun streamed through the windows of the house and down the long alleys between the buildings. Ali cautiously opened the door and stepped out. Abu Dhar followed a few paces behind him, treading carefully for fear of endangering both himself and his guide and losing the only chance he would have of reaching the man he had been longing to meet.

Abu Dhar kept his distance from Ali, pretending not to follow him, and watching carefully as he turned into one of the side streets. Finally, they reached the house where the Blessed Prophet was staying. Ali entered the house, and after a moment, Abu Dhar followed.

Abu Dhar saw in front of him a face the likes of which he had never seen before. The Blessed Prophet's face showed an inner light of peace and wisdom, of kindness and determination. It radiated a human warmth that he never knew existed.

Abu Dhar hesitated for a second, then moved forward a few steps and said: 'Peace be with you, O Messenger of God.'

'And peace be with you', replied the Blessed Prophet, 'and the mercy and blessings of God'.

Then slowly the Blessed Prophet began explaining to Abu Dhar. 'It is true, brother, that I am a Messenger of God, and my message is this: There is no God but Allah, He is your Lord and Creator, and to Him do we surrender. All other gods which people worship can neither harm nor benefit us. They cannot guide man nor advise him how to live. By accepting Allah as your only God, you will be freed from the yoke of all of them, from idolatry and slavery.' The Blessed Prophet then recited some verses of the Quran.

The moment Abu Dhar set eyes on the Blessed Prophet he made his decision. He was already disillusioned with the false gods which were being worshipped in Makka, the gods of stone and clay and the false gods of wealth, status and desire which reside within man. He had also come to hate the looting and plundering which he had once been so good at. So before leaving the Blessed Prophet's house, Abu Dhar became a Muslim by making his declaration of faith and declaring his belief in the One God and His Messenger.

During the days that followed, Abu Dhar was taught to perform the ablutions and to say the Prayers. He learned the basic tenets of Islam, was taught to speak the truth, to be honest in his dealings, to keep a promise, to fight oppression and injustice, to help the poor, orphans and widows, to spend money in the way of Allah, and to spread the message of God to everyone.

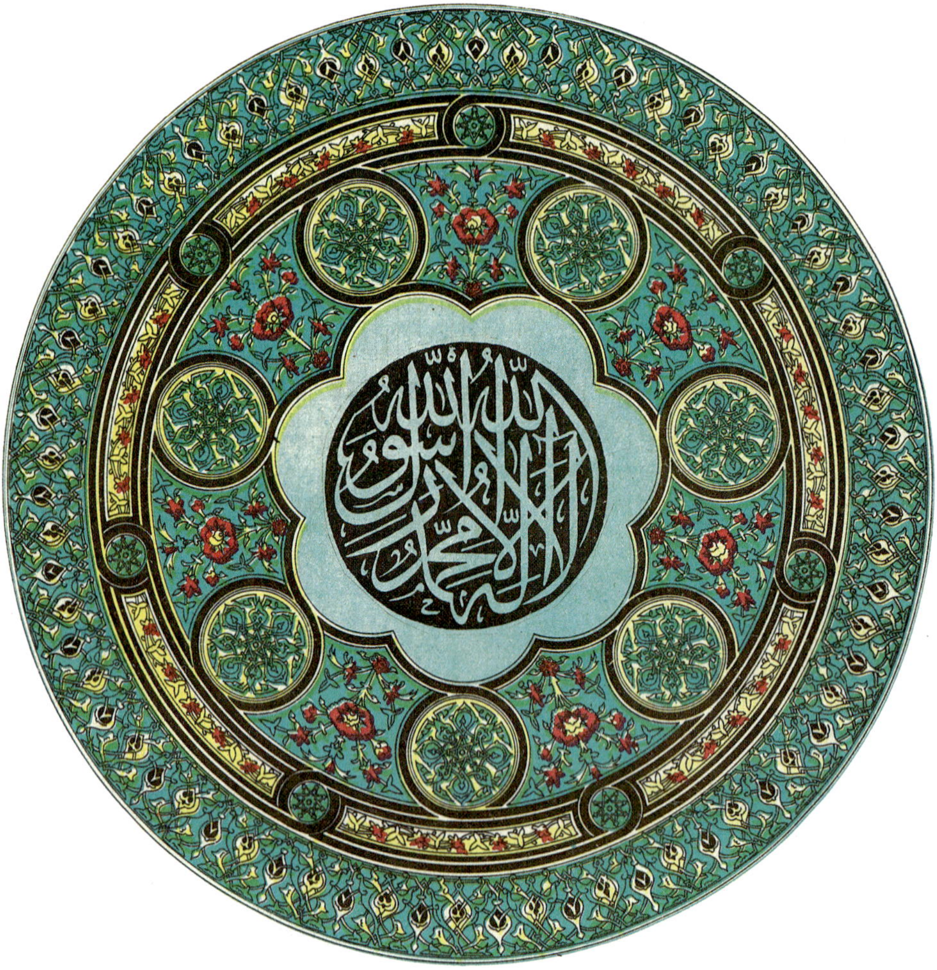
لا اله الا الله محمد رسول الله

When Abu Dhar arrived back in the valley of Waddan some nights later, he went straight to his brother's house and told him everything that had happened from the time he had left. All night long they discussed the meeting with Ali, and the visit to the Blessed Prophet. Anis was eager to hear all the details, especially the Blessed Prophet's words. Finally, Abu Dhar reached the part of the story where he had taken an active role in proving his allegiance:

Finally the Blessed Prophet said to me: 'It may be safer if you do not let anyone know that you have embraced Islam. People in Makka are still in opposition, and I fear that they might even go so far as to kill you if they found out.'

Well, even though I greatly valued the Blessed Prophet's advice, I was burning with desire to make it known to everyone that I had found the truth. So I answered him boldly: 'By the one who holds my soul in his hands, I shall not leave Makka until I have openly declared my conversion to Islam, to the Quraysh and to anyone who happens to hear me!'

The Blessed Prophet just smiled and kept silent. So, filled with a faith and courage such as I had never experienced before, I headed straight for the Haram,* and arriving there I walked boldly through the door. The members of the Quraysh were sitting in their usual places holding some sort of meeting. They paid no attention as I entered, but as soon as I began to

*The Mosque which surrounds the Ka'ba.

speak they stared at me, dumbfounded. 'Hear me, O members of the Quraysh!' I announced. 'If you would learn the truth, then pay close attention to my words. If you fear the fires of Hell, then follow my example! For on this day have I become a Muslim. I have declared my belief in the One God and in His Messenger, Muhammad, for He alone knows the truth. Know, then, that your idols are lies and will lead you to damnation. Amend your ways! Listen to Muhammad while there is still time . . .'

Before I could finish the sentence they seized me roughly; one held my arms while another struck me a blow across the face so that my words would be silenced. 'You dare enter our circle and address us in this manner!' one of them bellowed. Another became so enraged that he began beating me as hard as he could . . . I was sure that all the bones in my body were broken and that I would not escape alive.

Suddenly Abbas appeared upon the scene. We had met briefly at the house of the Blessed Prophet, and I learned later that although he had not embraced Islam he was secretly in sympathy with his nephew's message. I could see that he wanted to stop them from beating me . . . he was pulling on his beard and pursing his lips trying desperately to think of the right thing to say.

'Woe unto you all!' he cried out suddenly. 'Do you know who this man is? Think what you are doing! Think of the terrible consequences!'

Hearing Abbas, they stopped hitting me, but two of them still held me.

'This man', continued Abbas, 'is from the tribe of Ghifar. He lives right on the caravan route in the valley of Waddan! If you just follow your passions and injure or kill him, you can be sure his tribe will do the same to you! They'll plunder your caravans so you'll have nothing left but a pile of rags and broken pots.'

At this, the two men who were holding me grumbled, but marched me to the door and kicked me outside.

I glanced briefly at Abbas, and I am sure he was able to read the thanks in my eyes, for he looked down and stroked his whiskers with a smile.

So I picked myself up and walked painfully to the Blessed Prophet's house. I did not feel so courageous any more; rather, I was suffering more from the uselessness of my venture than from the blows I had received. When the Blessed Prophet saw me and heard what had happened, he put his hand on my shoulder and said: 'Didn't I advise you not to openly declare your conversion to Islam?'

I felt foolish and hung my head. 'O Messenger of God', I told him, 'I was convinced they would listen to me.'

'Brother', he answered, 'you are needed for more

important things than to receive unnecessary blows. Now go back to your people and inform them of what you have learned here. Call them to the One God, and, if Allah wills, they will hear you and believe in Islam, and later you will surely be rewarded. The time will come when my mission will succeed, when there will be no need to hide nor to fear persecution. When the time comes that you hear of this, then come and join me.'

Those were the last words he spoke to me, Anis. After that, I left with his blessing and Ali accompanied me to the edge of town.

Anis had been listening attentively to his brother's words. After a while he said, 'I know you have found the right way, brother. I too wish to testify as you have done, and after that we shall bring this news to our mother, and then to everyone in the tribe, and with God's grace their hearts will be touched and they will see the truth.'

And this is exactly what happened. Anis, Abu Dhar and their mother went from tent to tent, from house to house; they spoke of Islam in the market place, at weddings and at family gatherings, and little by little, one by one, the brotherhood of Islam grew amongst the members of the tribe until finally almost all were converted and became strong in their faith.